The Best Eid Ever

Asma Mobin-Uddin

Illustrated by Laura Jacobsen

BOYDS MILLS PRESS

HONESDALE, PENNSYLVANIA

The author wishes to thank Maliha Raazi and Shamsa Bashir Ali
for their gracious help and support.

Boyds Mills Press, Inc.
815 Church Street
Honesdale, Pennsylvania 18431
Printed in China

Library of Congress Cataloging-in-Publication Data

Mobin-Uddin, Asma.
The best Eid ever / Asma Mobin-Uddin ; illustrated by Laura Jacobsen.—1st ed.
p. cm.
ISBN 978-1-59078-431-0 (hardcover : alk. paper)
1. 'Id al-Adha—Juvenile literature. 2. Fasts and feasts—Islam—Juvenile literature.
I. Jacobsen, Laura, ill. II. Title.

BP186.45.M63 2007
297.3'6—dc22
2006037945

First edition
The text of this book is set in 13-point Minion.
The illustrations are done in pastel pencil.

10 9 8 7 6 5 4 3 2 1

For my mother
—A.M.-U.

For Craig
—L.J.

$\mathcal{A}$NEESA SAT IN HER BED, looking out the window. Her parents were away at the Hajj pilgrimage and she missed them. Saudi Arabia was so far from her home in America.

She thought about last year's Eid holiday. When she had worn her new *shalwar kameez*, with flowery orange henna designs on her hands, Daddy had said she looked just like a princess. Mommy had let her eat candy before breakfast. They all went to Eid prayers together and then visited friends all day. But today the house was quiet.

Just then, Aneesa's grandmother bustled into the room.

"ANEESA, HAPPY EID!" NONNI SAT
on the bed and greeted her granddaughter with a big hug and kiss.
"Time to get ready for prayers." Aneesa returned the hug and then
slumped back on the bed.

"Why the sad face, my dear?" Nonni gently brushed the hair
out of Aneesa's eyes. "Do you miss Mommy and Daddy?"

Aneesa nodded. She felt like she might cry.

"I know it's hard without your parents here," Nonni said.
"But please don't be sad, today of all days. We'll have fun
together, just you and me, OK?"

Aneesa tried to smile. She didn't want her grandmother to
feel bad. "OK," she said as Nonni stood up and walked over to
the closet.

"Now I have a surprise for you." Nonni lifted up a blanket
on the closet shelf and pulled out a gift-wrapped box that had
been hidden underneath it.

ANEESA PULLED THE RIBBON OFF THE BOX and opened it. Her eyes lit up as she saw the beautiful Eid clothes from Pakistan. Pulling out the *kurta* on top, she ran her fingers over the soft, shimmering fabric and its gold embroidery and shiny sequins. Purple and gold bangles clinked together as Nonni unwrapped them. Handmade Pakistani shoes, tucked in tissue paper, still lay in the box.

"Nonni, I love my new Eid clothes! How did you know purple was my favorite color? Thank you!" Aneesa hugged her grandmother. "I can't wait to get dressed."

"There's still more," Nonni said, smiling, as she pulled a bright red *shalwar kameez* and a silky yellow *gharara* out of the box. Each outfit had matching bangles and shoes.

"There are three sets of clothes, one for each of the three days of Eid. Now, which one do you want to wear to prayers this morning?"

"The purple one!"

Nonni smiled. "It will look beautiful on you. I'll iron it while you're getting ready. But first, I have to stir the lamb korma."

"ℒAMB KORMA!" ANEESA jumped out of bed and ran to the kitchen. The aroma of her favorite dinner cooking on the stove made her mouth water. "Please, can I taste some?" Nonni scooped out a spoonful of bubbling lamb curry, blew on it, made sure it wasn't too hot, and then gave Aneesa a taste. Aneesa savored the salty, spicy curry in her mouth. "Yum! It's good."

"I'm glad you like it. Now let's hurry and get ready so we're not late for the prayers."

$\mathcal{A}$T THE PRAYER HALL, THE IMAM GAVE
a sermon about the Hajj pilgrimage. Aneesa had a hard time
paying attention because she kept thinking about her parents
and wishing they were with her.

After the sermon ended, the women and children in the
women's section of the prayer hall folded their prayer rugs
and greeted each other. Aneesa hugged so many people!
The doughnuts on the back tables were quickly finished.

ANEESA NOTICED TWO YOUNG GIRLS standing alone, watching the excitement around them. The older girl's *hijab* was torn. The younger girl's dress fell almost to the floor, and she kept her arms bent so her sleeves wouldn't slip down over her hands.

Aneesa walked over to them. "Why didn't you wear your Eid clothes today?" she asked.

The older girl stared shyly at the floor

Seeing that her sister was not going to answer, the younger girl blurted out, "We don't have new clothes this Eid. We had to leave all our stuff and run away when a fire burned our house down."

The older girl turned toward her sister. "Mariam, we have to be thankful the war can't get us now. We are safe and we are together. Papa says God will give us whatever we need."

"I wish Papa were here with us now. But ever since we came to America, he always has to work," Mariam told Aneesa. "He even had to work on Eid! But later he's going to bring Zayneb and me candy, and we're going to the mosque together for the afternoon prayers."

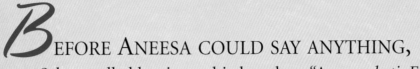

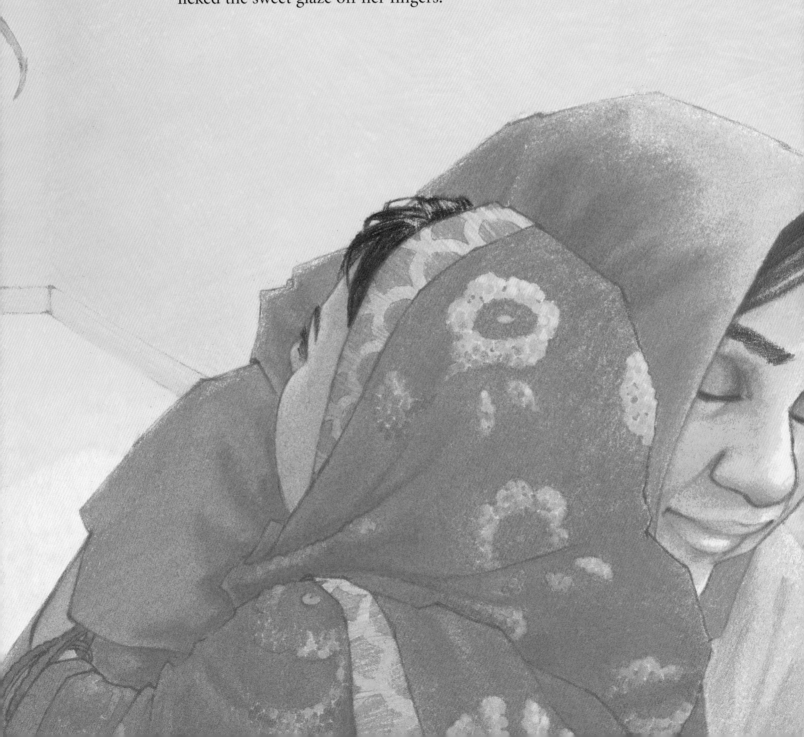

*B*EFORE ANEESA COULD SAY ANYTHING,
Aunty Selma pulled her into a big bear hug. "Aneesa, *beti, Eid Mubarak!* My dear, Happy Eid! You look so pretty, *masha'Allah*, as God has willed. You and your nonni come and visit me today, OK?"

Aneesa was swept up by other aunties and friends in hugs, kisses, and greetings. While hugging Aunty Barak, Aneesa saw Mariam pick up a piece of doughnut off the floor. The girl looked around quickly. Then she put the doughnut piece into her mouth and licked the sweet glaze off her fingers.

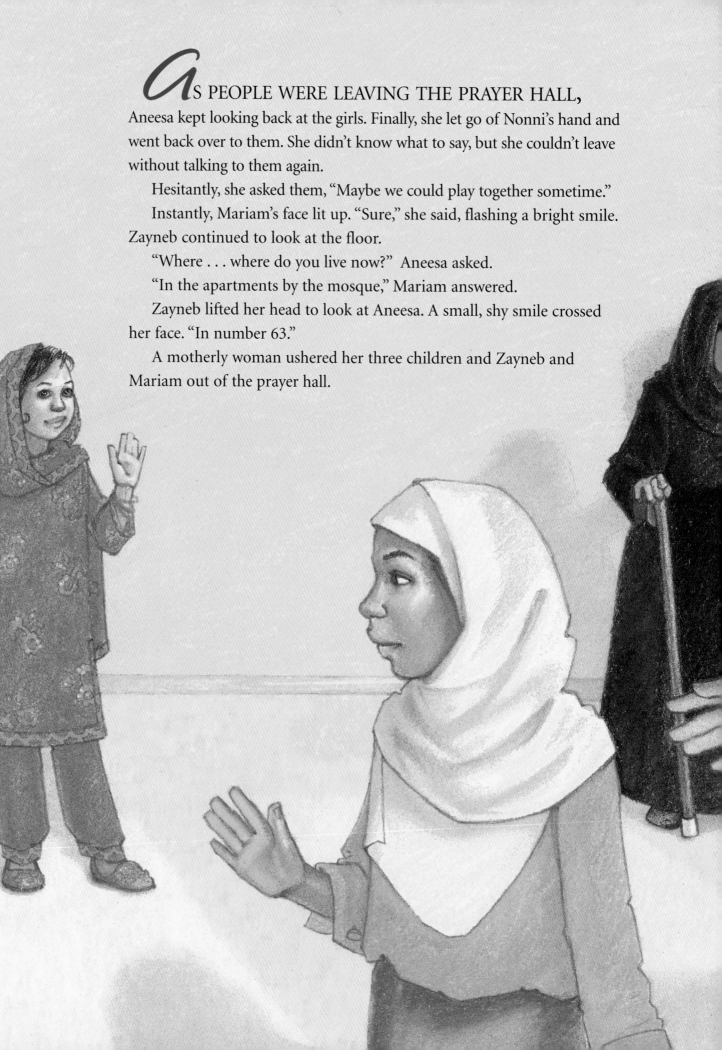

As PEOPLE WERE LEAVING THE PRAYER HALL,
Aneesa kept looking back at the girls. Finally, she let go of Nonni's hand and
went back over to them. She didn't know what to say, but she couldn't leave
without talking to them again.

Hesitantly, she asked them, "Maybe we could play together sometime."

Instantly, Mariam's face lit up. "Sure," she said, flashing a bright smile.
Zayneb continued to look at the floor.

"Where . . . where do you live now?" Aneesa asked.

"In the apartments by the mosque," Mariam answered.

Zayneb lifted her head to look at Aneesa. A small, shy smile crossed
her face. "In number 63."

A motherly woman ushered her three children and Zayneb and
Mariam out of the prayer hall.

$\mathcal{A}$T HOME THAT AFTERNOON WHILE NONNI was heating up the food for dinner, Aneesa told her about the girls she had met.

Nonni listened quietly. "Sometimes when families leave their homes because of war or other bad problems, they have to leave behind everything they own," Nonni told her. "Many families have come to America as refugees, looking for a safe, good place for their children to live and grow up."

"Does God help these families?"

"Of course, my dear. God helps everyone." Nonni was stirring the curry. "But sometimes not in the way you might think. Instead of just taking away the bad times, He might send good people to help them through the bad times. Meanwhile, the families have to work hard and trust that God's help is always near."

Nonni opened the oven door to check on the *roti*. "Do you remember the story of Prophet Abraham, his wife, Hajar, and their baby, Ismail?"

Aneesa nodded. Mommy and Daddy had told her that many of the lessons of the Hajj pilgrimage were based on this story. Prophet Abraham's family trusted in God, even in very difficult times, and God always took care of them.

Nonni and Aneesa said a prayer for Zayneb and Mariam's family. Then Aneesa told Nonni about a plan she had made.

_L_ATER THAT AFTERNOON, AS SHADOWS LENGTHENED across the city, Muslim families were leaving the mosque after praying the _Asr_ prayer.

"Aneesa, sit quietly. Someone will hear you," Nonni whispered to her granddaughter as they crouched behind the bushes outside the apartment building next to the mosque. "Here they come. Duck down!"

Through the leaves, they saw the two girls and a man stop in front of the decorated baskets neatly arranged on the cracked stoop in front of their door. "What's this?" In surprise, the man read the attached card. "Happy Eid to Mariam, Zayneb, and their papa."

Aneesa felt as if she might burst with excitement. Would they like the presents? Zayneb and Mariam opened the baskets.

"Wow, beautiful clothes! Look at all the sparkles on this yellow shirt."

"What a pretty red outfit—with matching bangles and shoes!"

"I can't believe this," the man said softly. "Lamb and chicken, rice and vegetables. Even desserts and candy. Who could have left all this?"

"Papa, help us carry the baskets inside!" Mariam was trying to drag a basket across the sidewalk.

"Put them down, girls," their father commanded. "We don't take charity."

*T*HEIR FATHER PAUSED. Then Mariam asked
softly, "But can I keep the yellow clothes? I love yellow. And what
about these sparkly bangles?"

"No, my dears." Their father spoke again. "You know that
a Muslim does not beg from others."

"But Papa, we didn't ask for them," Zayneb pointed out.

Papa didn't budge. "I will provide for my family.
There are other people who need this food and these
clothes more than we do. Now let's go."

"Can I just eat this cookie right now?"

Aneesa could hardly breathe. What if they
didn't take the gifts? As she leaned forward to
see better, a twig snapped under her.

"What was that noise?" the father
asked as he turned around to face the
bushes. Aneesa and Nonni ducked as
his heavy footsteps approached
their hiding place.

*T*HROUGH THE LEAVES, ANEESA COULD SEE
the man's stern features and firmly set chin coming toward
them. Hidden behind thick eyebrows were soft, gentle eyes.
In these eyes, Aneesa recognized the same look of tenderness
she often saw in her own father's face.

Aneesa and the man looked at each other for a long
moment. Then, abruptly, he turned around and walked back
to his daughters.

$\mathcal{H}$E KNELT DOWN ON ONE KNEE and opened his arms. The girls wrapped their arms around him, and Mariam climbed onto his knee. "Papa, there's more food than we need here," she said, small fingers gently touching his cheek. "Why don't we share it with the neighbors?"

"And please can we keep the pretty Eid clothes? Please?" asked Zayneb.

Aneesa saw the man's face soften as he drew his daughters close to him. As he hugged them, he nodded. And he smiled at Aneesa and Nonni.

$\mathcal{A}$FTER ANEESA AND NONNI RETURNED HOME, Nonni picked up the telephone and dialed. "Hello, I'd like to order a medium vegetable pizza for delivery," she said. After she hung up, she shook her head. "Eating pizza on Eid. My child, I have never had an Eid like this one."

"Me neither," Aneesa said. "I can't wait to tell Mommy and Daddy about it!"

Later in the evening, as Aneesa and Nonni snuggled up on the couch and ate pizza, they both agreed—this had been the best Eid ever!

Author's Notes

Hajj Pilgrimage. Islam's Hajj pilgrimage is one of the largest annual religious gatherings in the world. Millions of people make this sacred journey to sites in and near Mecca in present-day Saudi Arabia each year to worship God and seek His mercy and forgiveness. Adult Muslims must make the pilgrimage at least once in their lives if they are physically and financially able. Many of the rituals of Hajj relate to the experiences of the Prophet Abraham and his family.

Eid al-Adha. There are two main Muslim holidays. Eid al-Fitr is the holiday just after the month of Ramadan. Eid al-Adha, the holiday in this story, is a celebration that occurs at the end of the Hajj pilgrimage. It honors the Prophet Abraham's steadfastness, obedience, and love for God because he was willing to sacrifice his only son in obedience to God's command. When it was clear that Abraham had passed this difficult test from God, a ram was substituted for sacrifice instead of the boy. This story is told in both the Qur'an and the Bible, although some of the details differ. The lesson of the holiday is that people should love God more than anything else in their lives.

Abraham, Hagar, and Ishmael. The transliterated forms of these names as they are pronounced in the Arabic language are Ibrahim, Hajar, and Ismail. According to Muslim understanding, the Prophet Abraham saw in a vision that he was to leave his second wife, Hagar, and their infant son in the desert. When her provisions ran out, Hagar, alone in the desert with her thirsty, crying infant, ran back and forth between two hills searching for water and praying for help. God caused a spring to gush forth near the infant, providing life-saving water and care for the mother and her child.

One of the central rites of the Hajj pilgrimage is the reenactment of Hagar running back and forth between the hills of Safa and Marwa, trusting in God and remembering that God's loving sustenance and provision always come. Hajj pilgrims drink from the water of the well of Zamzam, the same spring God established to answer Hagar's prayers.

Chapter 21 of the biblical book of Genesis also mentions God providing a well of water for Hagar and Ishmael in the desert. Other details in the biblical account differ from those in the Islamic tradition.

Glossary

Aneesa (Uh-NEE-suh)

Asr (UH-sr) prayers — the late afternoon prayer, the third of the five daily Muslim prayers

Beti (BAY-tee) — Urdu word for "daughter," used as a term of affection

Eid Mubarak (EED moo-BAR-uk) — typical Eid greeting that means "Blessings of Eid." Eid can also be spelled 'Id.

Ghararah (gha-RAH-rah) — festive South Asian clothing that resembles a long skirt but has a separate section for each leg

Hijab (hij-JAB) — a headcovering worn by Muslim girls and women for modesty

Imam (i-MAAM) — Muslim prayer leader

Kurta (KUR-tah) — a tuniclike shirt

Masha'Allah (mah-SHAH-ul-LAH) — Arabic phrase meaning "as God has willed," used to express appreciation

Nonni (NON-nee) — Urdu word for "maternal grandmother"

Roti (RO-tee) — a flat, round bread

Shalwar kameez (shul-VAR ka-MEEZ) — South Asian clothing that resembles a long shirt and baggy pants